I0788099

The author acknowledges the people of the **Dharawal** and **Dhurga** language groups as the traditional owners of the lands within the boundaries of **Bundanon** and recognises their continuous connection to culture, community and Country.

In **Dharawal** the word **Bundanon** means deep valley.

Always was, always will be.

How to read this book

bold

not bold

Names are written in **bold.**

The pictures help you understand the words.

Lennie's gift

by **Casey Gray**

It is the middle of the night.

Dip cannot sleep.

She is at the hut

where writers go to write.

She should be writing a book

but she feels stressed.

She has no ideas for a story.

Dip hears a door creak open.

Her heart thumps.

She yells

Who is there?

Boom.

Boom.

Boom.

A chair falls in the wind

bang!

Dip takes a big calm breath.

Maybe the wind opened the door.

She tip toes to close the door

but there is a kangaroo

with eyes like blue opals.

Opals are colourful rocks.

It hops away.

Boing.

Boing.

Boing.

Dip follows.

Frogs sing.

The dirt path shines

with butterflies

that glow in the dark.

They land on **Dip's**

- arms

- and face

- and hands.

They leave gold dust on her skin.

The kangaroo hops into the bush.

And is gone

poof!

Dip is lost in the dark.

Mozzies bite.

Dip cries.

A tall lady comes out of the fog.

Her eyes look like blue opals.

As the lady gets closer

Dip feels better.

Warmer.

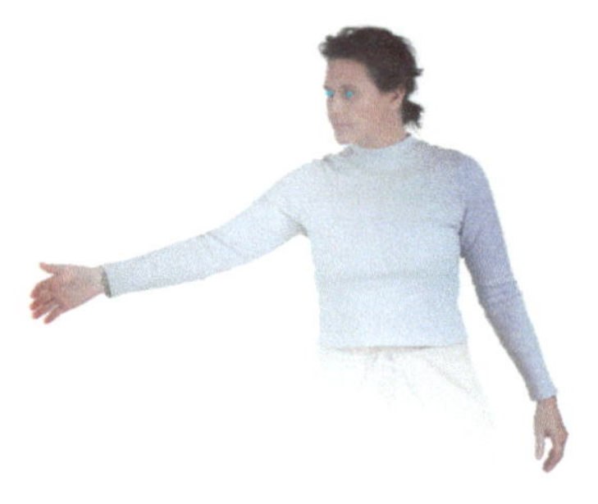

The lady says

Come with me.

She holds **Dip's** hand.

They walk over hills

and step over dead trees.

The lady says

I sit by the river

and write stories.

One story is about the river.

The river turns into a slow blue snake.

I used to sneak away from my

busy home

to find a quiet place to write.

Now I walk this place

to stop the plants getting stolen

and to keep the animals safe from people with guns.

Now I have lots of time to write.

Dip says

I have time to write

but I have no idea what to write about.

The lady says

Dip close your eyes.

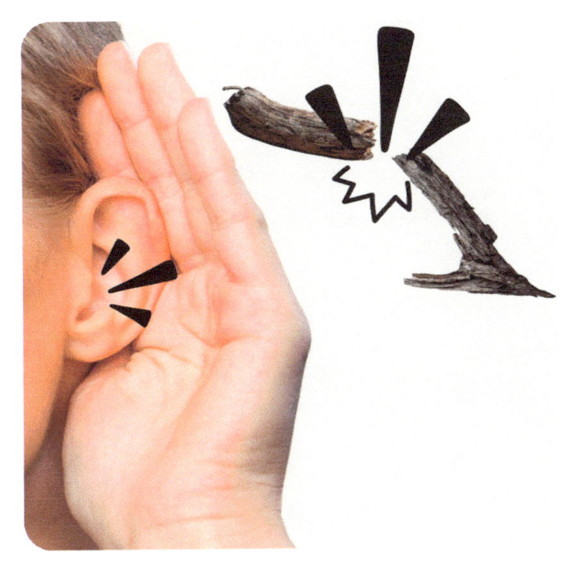

Hear the sticks crackle

as the wombats waddle.

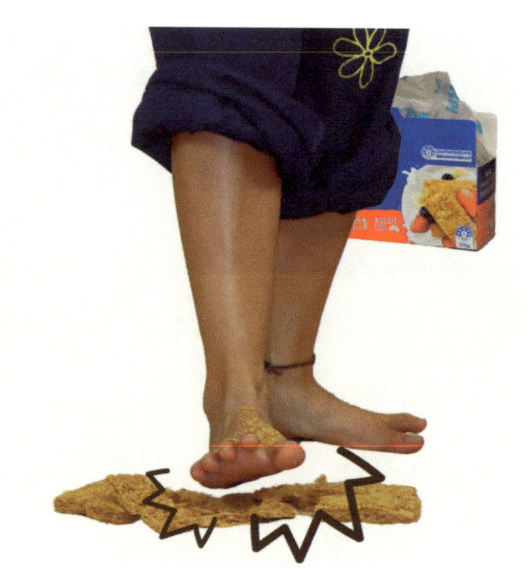

It sounds like crunching **Weet-Bix** with your feet.

Now **Dip**

look up.

Look at the star dust.

Think about what the dust can

see in space

like the stars exploding.

The lady asks

Dip what can you smell.

Gum leaves.

The lady asks

What else can you smell.

Dip says

Roo poo.

Dip says

Roo poo reminds me of camping

with my brother.

He put it in my sleeping bag

so I threw the poo at the

rascal's head.

The lady says

That is the start of a good story.

Then **Dip** sees a big old house.

She runs to it.

Past a sign that says

Haunted Loop Bush Walk.

An alarm goes off.

Dip's ears hurt.

A man shines a torch in her face.

He is the man who looks after the house.

He turns the alarm off.

He says

I thought you were a robber.

Dip tells the man about being lost

and about the lady who saved her.

Dip turns to say thank you

but the lady is gone

poof!

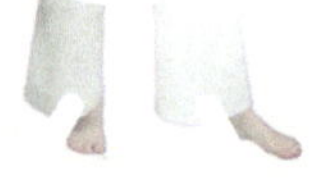

The man says

I think you had a visit from the ghost.

People say a ghost lives in

the writer's hut.

The man says

And I think it is the ghost of **Lennie Boyd**.

I think **Lennie** will never stop caring for

- the plants

- the animals

- and artists like you **Dip**.

But keep that a secret.

Dip skips back to the writer's hut

as the sun comes up

excited to use **Lennie's** gift.

Ideas for stories are all around us.

You just need to find them.

Yvonne Boyd *in Tuscany*, c1973, photographer unknown. Bundanon Archive.

A page to say thank you

The world would be a better place if everyone had a **Janey**. I love and appreciate you.

Thank you to **Accessible Arts NSW** and **Bundanon** for having me as artist in residence and inspiring me to write this story.

Thank you to fellow artist in residence **Lulu Wulf**, your creative and adventurous gold hexagon filtered soul I am lucky to have happened across.

Thank you to the people who tested this book to see if it is easy and fun to read.

Casey Gray Bundanon Writer's Cottage, 2022.

Information about the printing of this book

Lennie's gift: Easy Read

Author: **Casey Gray**

Published by **Books By ED**